Adam

MW01127806

Spread   kindness

♡ Emma Wolf

May I Sit At Your Table?

by Grace A. Wolf
illustrated by Samuel J. Gross

May I Sit At Your Table? by Grace A. Wolf
Copyright © 2023 by Grace A. Wolf

ISBNs
Hardcover: 979-8-9887809-0-8
Paperback: 979-8-9887809-1-5
eBook: 979-8-9887809-2-2

All rights reserved. No portion of this book may be reproduced in any form without permission from the publisher, except as permitted by U.S. copyright law. For permissions, contact: gwolfbooks@gmail.com

Cover and Interior Design by Carolyn Vaughan:
cvaughandesigns.com
cvaughandesigns@gmail.com

Printed in the United States.

Dedication

To my brother Sam who is so much kinder to the world
than the world is to him.

In the small town of Sunwoody lived a wonderful little girl named Abby.

Abby was Deaf, but that did not make her any less curious or excited about the world.

Abby did not use her voice. Instead, she had a superpower—her hands could talk! Abby could twist, twirl, and move her hands and fingers in different ways to show her thoughts and feelings.

It was magical how Abby used these movements to create words. This special way of talking is called **sign language**.

Abby went to a nearby elementary school where there were no other Deaf children, and no one knew how to sign. When people were talking, Abby had to closely watch their lips move and guess what words they were saying. This is called **lipreading** but it's very hard to do.

Even though it was hard, it was important to Abby that she attend the same school as all the other children in her neighborhood so that she could learn and make friends.

The school was a place full of joy and laughter,
especially at lunchtime.

That is when all the kids gathered around tables
to eat sandwiches, share their stories,
and enjoy their friends.

Abby did not have fun during lunch. She always sat by herself because no one ever invited her to sit at their table.

The children simply did not understand why Abby did not talk or seem to hear things. She did not laugh at their jokes or join in their games. They thought she was different and so they left her alone.

One day after returning home from school, Abby could no longer hold in her feelings. She burst into tears, letting her parents know how alone she felt, especially at lunchtime.

Abby's wise parents lovingly sat her down
to give her some advice. They told her to be
brave and simply ask her classmates if she
could sit with them.

The following day, Abby walked up to a table full of kids with a hopeful smile. She signed, "May I sit at your table?" and pointed to an empty seat.

The entire table looked at her, their faces full of confusion. They did not understand her hand movements. Some of them giggled, others just looked away.

No one invited her to sit with them.

Abby ran out of the lunchroom, ashamed and embarrassed, with tears streaming down her face.

At home, Abby shared her painful story
with her parents.
They hugged her tightly, reminded her how
loved she was, and said they felt awful for
what had happened to her.

Even with her parents' comforting words, Abby kept replaying the horrible events of the lunchroom in her mind. She felt hopeless and thought that she would never have any friends.

Abby was so upset that she did not want to return to school the next day, and her parents allowed her to stay home.

Back at school, an amazing teacher named Ms. Baker had watched the entire lunch scene unfold. She saw Abby's brave attempt to join the children and the hurtful way they had reacted.
Ms. Baker knew that she had to do something.

That evening, she studied as much as she could about Deaf culture and sign language.

Abby was not in school the next day, and Ms. Baker understood why.

She gathered all the children for a special lesson. Ms. Baker started by telling them about people who are Deaf, like Abby. She explained how they use their hands to talk with sign language.

She showed them how to sign words like "Hello," "Thank you," and "Friend."

Ms. Baker also explained that during class, she made a special effort to face Abby and to speak more slowly so that Abby could read her lips.

Most importantly, Ms. Baker taught them to be accepting of someone who is different and that everyone should be included and treated nicely.

After this lesson, the children felt sorry that they had made Abby feel so excluded, and after school, a group of them got together to learn as many words in sign language as they could.

The next day, at the encouragement
of her parents,
Abby returned to school.

During lunchtime, Abby walked into the
lunchroom and sat alone,
just like she always did.

But this time,
something amazing happened.

A group of her classmates
came up to her and signed,

"May we sit at your table?"

Abby's heart filled with joy
as her new friends sat down to join her.

From that day forward,
Abby always had a welcoming place to sit
and friends to share her lunch with.

Each day, Ms. Baker taught the class a few more words in sign language. The kids looked forward to these lessons. They practiced with each other and even tried signing with Abby.

When talking to Abby, they also took special care to face her and to speak slowly.

The next time you are at school, and you see someone sitting alone, remember Abby. Do not be afraid to reach out and include them. Even the smallest act of kindness can make a big difference.

In the end, Abby's story is not just about how to thoughtfully treat someone who is Deaf; it is about understanding, accepting, and including everyone, no matter how they communicate or what makes them different.

The End

Acknowledgements

Thank you to my parents for truly believing that I could do anything I set my mind to.

Thank you to my friend Abby Hoelscher for always being there for me and for helping make the American Sign Language Club a success.

Thank you to my Clayton High School ASL Club sponsor Joyce Bell for taking the time to support and guide our ASL club.

Thank you to all of my teachers at Clayton High School who provided a dynamic academic environment that consistently pushed me to strive for excellence.

A very special thanks to my guidance counselor, Tobie Smith, who has been my rock throughout high school.

Thank you to Carolyn Vaughan for recognizing the book's potential to make positive change, never doubting me and providing me guidance in the many steps required to publish this book.

About the Author

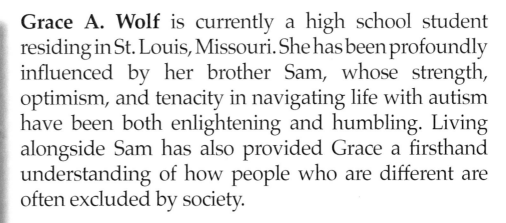

Grace A. Wolf is currently a high school student residing in St. Louis, Missouri. She has been profoundly influenced by her brother Sam, whose strength, optimism, and tenacity in navigating life with autism have been both enlightening and humbling. Living alongside Sam has also provided Grace a firsthand understanding of how people who are different are often excluded by society.

Passionate about spreading awareness, understanding, and acceptance, Grace has poured her heart into crafting children's books where she encourages her young readers to extend friendship and acceptance to those of diverse backgrounds and abilities. She is firmly committed to laying the groundwork for a more compassionate society, one book at a time.

About the Illustrator

Samuel J. Gross is an illustrator who brings stories to life. Diagnosed with autism at the age of 3, Sam discovered his love for art before he even uttered his first word. Sam's resilience in overcoming the challenges presented by his journey with autism, coupled with his distinct creativity, enables him to infuse a unique vitality into every character he creates. Sam is the loving older brother of Grace A. Wolf.

Artistic color enhancement provided by Grace A. Wolf.

Printed in the USA
CPSIA information can be obtained
at www.ICGtesting.com
JSRC081602270823
47315JS00001B/1

9798988780908